For
Nicholas

The Very Silly Mayor

by Tom Tomorrow

 Brooklyn
New York

Printed in China
10 9 8 7 6 5 4 3 2 1

Design by Dan Perkins
Layout by Keith Campbell

Ig Publishing
178 Clinton Avenue
Brooklyn, NY 11205

Library of Congress Cataloging-in-Publication Data

Tomorrow, Tom, 1961-
 The very silly mayor / by Tom Tomorrow.
    p. cm.
 Summary: When the mayor of a pretty good, medium-sized city
begins to make decisions that are not only silly but dangerous, as
well, Sparky the penguin is the only citizen willing to speak out.
 ISBN-13: 978-1-935439-01-1
 ISBN-10: 1-935439-01-4
 [1. Citizenship--Fiction. 2. Mayors--Fiction. 3. Penguins--Fiction.]
I. Title.
 PZ7.T5978Ver 2009
 [E]--dc22
                                    2009007041

Once there was a penguin named Sparky, who lived in a medium-sized house in a medium-sized city with his best friend Blinky, a very nice dog.

It was a pretty good city, but it had a very silly mayor with some very silly ideas.

One day, for instance, the mayor decided that all the police officers in the medium-sized city should wear clown costumes, with big red noses and big goofy clown shoes.

Another day, he ordered the firefighters of the medium-
sized city to put out fires with peanut butter instead of
water.

And on yet another day, he decreed that all the houses in the city should be painted with green and purple stripes.

Sparky the penguin was not happy at all.

"Police officers should not have to wear clown costumes," Sparky said. "And you cannot put out fires with peanut butter."

"And what if people do not want to paint their houses with green and purple stripes?" he asked. "This mayor has some very silly ideas!"

Blinky, being a
very nice dog,
tried to think of
something nice
to say.

"Green and
purple are very
bright colors!"
he said.

Later Sparky turned on the TV. "I'll bet people are very mad," he said. But to his surprise, a man on TV said, "I think clown costumes for the police are a great idea!"

Another man on TV said, "Peanut butter sounds like a delicious way to fight fires!"

And a woman said, "I can't wait to paint my house with green and purple stripes!" Sparky could not believe his ears.

Sparky went out and bought a newspaper.
The headline said:

Sparky could not believe his eyes.

Sparky's neighbor, Biff, was busy painting his house with green and purple stripes. "Hey there, Sparky," said Biff. "When are you going to start painting your house green and purple?"

"Never," said Sparky. "It is a very silly idea."

"But— but— " Biff sounded confused. "It was the mayor's idea!"

"Sometimes mayors have silly ideas," said Sparky.

"Do you really want your house to be painted green and purple?" Sparky asked.

"It might not have been my first choice," admitted Biff.

"Then why are you doing it?" asked Sparky.

"Because everyone else is doing it too," said Biff. "I don't want anyone to laugh at me."

"It's true," said another neighbor. "We're all doing it!" Sparky sighed.

Just then a bank robber ran by. Sparky knew he was a
bank robber because he was wearing what bank robbers
always wear: a mask, a striped shirt, and shoes that were
good for running. And of course, he was carrying a big
bag with a dollar sign on it.

After he was out of sight, a policeman appeared. He was trying to chase the bank robber, but the big clown shoes he was wearing made it hard to run. "I give up," the policeman said. "How am I supposed to chase bank robbers when I have to wear these clown shoes?"

"Why don't you put your police uniform back on?" asked Sparky.

"Because all the other police officers are wearing clown costumes," said the policeman. "I don't want them to laugh at me."

Blinky couldn't think of anything nice to say about the clown costume, so he stayed quiet.

Suddenly they all smelled smoke. As luck would have it, Biff's house had caught on fire while they were talking.

"No problem," said the policeman. "I'll call the fire department on my radio."

And he did.

SNIFF!
SNIFF!

UH OH!

The firefighters showed up right away, but since the mayor had told them to put out fires with peanut butter instead of water, they weren't very helpful. "Peanut butter is delicious,"

said one fireman, "but it is not very useful for putting out fires." Sparky sighed again, and got his garden hose and put out the fire before it could do very much damage.

"I think we should all go visit the mayor," said Sparky. Biff and the policemen and the firemen and Blinky all agreed. So everyone climbed into the fire truck and rode downtown to City Hall.

They marched into the mayor's office and Sparky said, "Mister Mayor, you have some very silly ideas! Police officers cannot catch criminals if they have to wear clown suits! Firefighters cannot put out fires with peanut butter! And people do not want to paint their houses with green and purple stripes!"

"Why didn't someone tell me this sooner?" demanded the mayor.

A woman who worked in the mayor's office said, "Everyone else seemed to think they were good ideas! I didn't want anyone to laugh at me!"

"That's what I was afraid of, too!" said a man.

Sparky said, "So nobody thought they were good ideas — but you were all too afraid of being laughed at to say anything?"

"That pretty much sums it up," said the policeman in the clown costume.

Then the mayor made a surprise announcement.
"I am not a very good mayor," he said. "I am quitting and making Sparky the new mayor instead!"

"That's a great idea," said everyone in the room except for Sparky.

"You can't just quit and make a penguin mayor," he said. "You have to have an election!"

Everyone was quiet for a minute.

"We didn't really think it was a good idea," said a fireman at last. "We were just afraid of being laughed at."

The mayor said, "Okay, I have another idea — and this time, I think it really is a good one. I'll keep being mayor, Sparky, but I want you to work for me — because I know you will always tell me what you think, and you won't worry about people laughing at you."

"Okay," said Sparky. "As long as police officers can start wearing police uniforms again, and firefighters can put out fires with water again, and nobody has to paint their houses green and purple unless they want to."

"Consider it done," said the mayor.

And so the police were able to catch bank robbers again…

...and the firefighters were able to put out fires again...

...and the people who lived in the medium-sized city were able to paint their houses whatever colors they wanted.

"Now," said the mayor. "I have an idea! What if we build all the new buildings in our city out of candy? What do you think, Sparky?"

Sparky said, "I think I'm going to be very busy here."

And he was!